Say Hello To Apollo Rollo Rowe

by Gregory Moore Jr.

illustrated by Aaliyah Delrosario

Acknowledgements

First, I want to give thanks to God for His blessings. I would
also like to thank my loving wife, Marlene for her continuous
encouragement and support. I want to send a big thanks to my
children, grandchildren, and my little cousins as they are the inspiration
behind this book and others that will follow. I would like to send a heartfelt
thanks to my mother- Kathrine Bass, may she rest well in heaven,
my stepmother – Roberta Ladson, my father- Gregory Sr., my brothers, sisters,
and to the rest of my family. And finally, I would like to send a special thanks
to my close friends Kieth and Lynell Rowe, Albis "Chico" Del Rosario and his talented
daughter Aaliyah for making my dream of becoming an author come to reality
with the help of her illustrations.

-GMJ

I am so thankful to have had the opportunity to work on
Say Hello To Apollo Rollo Rowe. I do not think this opportunity would be possible
without having God and His constant guidence and provided blessings so I
must thank Him for this chance. I also would like to thank Gregory Moore Jr. for
entrusting me with illustrating his passion project along
with my family and friends who have always been supportive of my art goals.
I would not be where I am today without their
kind words and encouragement.

-AD

Adrianne Aaliyah is new to the area. She found nothing scarier than making new friends. So, one day at school, she used show-and-share to help her introduce herself and her dog.

Although she was shy, she gave it a try, and this is what she said:

"My name is Adrianne Aaliyah and I want you to say hello to Apollo Rollo Rowe."

He plays in the grass.

He plays in the sand.

He plays in the street.

And he loves to play in the snow.

He runs fast, faster, and he is the fastest dog on our block.

Apollo Rollo Rowe
Apollo Rollo Rowe

Apollo Rollo Rowe is a handsome dog.

9

He loves to bathe.

And he loves to be combed.

He is beautiful, more beautiful,
and he is the most beautiful dog
on our block.

Apollo Rollo Rowe
Apollo Rollo Rowe

Apollo Rollo Rowe is a loyal dog.

He comes when he is called.

Apollo!

And he loves to play fetch.

He is clever, cleverer, and he
is the cleverest dog on our block.

Apollo Rollo Rowe
Apollo Rollo Rowe

Apollo Rollo Rowe is a good guard dog.

17

He saves me from stranger danger
even if he is small.

18

His bark is **big**, **bigger**, and he
has the **biggest** bark on our block.

Apollo Rollo Rowe
Apollo Rollo Rowe

Apollo Rollo Rowe is a nice dog.

20

He loves to play and be pet by kids.

21

He is kind, kinder, and he is the
kindest dog on our block.

So, when Adrianne Aaliyah was done, and the kids said that they had fun,

she allowed all of them to come up and pet Apollo Rollo Rowe one-by-one.

23

After Adrianne Aaliyah's playful introduction, she was no longer worried and felt welcomed by her new classmates. She stood tall and with a great big smile, she ended by saying:

"So now you know. My name is Adrianne Aaliyah, and this is my dog, Apollo Rollo Rowe."

The End.

About the Author

Gregory Moore Jr., a Philadelphia native, is a devoted husband, father, and grandfather. He is a veteran who served honorably in the United States Army and in the United States Marine Corps. He received his master's degree in education and counseling from Norfolk State University and received his bachelor's degree in psychology from East Carolina University. While he has had a longing to write children's books over the years, now that he is a grandfather, he feels like it is the perfect time to bring his dream to fruition.

Say Hello to Apollo Rollo Rowe is a fun-loving, catchy, rhythmic, and educational children's book full of sight words, articulation, and repetition. It introduces this small, adorable, and adventurous dog named Apollo Rollo Rowe and his lovable partner, Adrianne Aaliyah, to the world.

Currently, he is in the process of writing children's books that will feature Apollo Rollo Rowe's adventures, highlight Adrianne Aaliyah and her bicultural family lessons, and more.